SpongeBob's
BOOK of
EXCUSES

Based on the TV series SpongeBob SquarePants
created by Stephen Hillenburg as seen on Nickelodeon

SIMON AND SCHUSTER
First published in Great Britain in 2006 by Simon & Schuster UK Ltd
Africa House, 64-78 Kingsway, London WC2B 6AH

Originally published in the USA in 2005 by Simon Spotlight,
an imprint of Simon & Schuster Children's Division, New York.

Book design by Lissi Erwin

A CIP catalogue record for this book is
available from the British Library

ISBN-13 978-1-4169-1676-5

Printed in Great Britain

3 5 7 9 10 8 6 4

SpongeBob's BOOK OF EXCUSES

by Holly Kowitt

SIMON AND SCHUSTER
/Nickelodeon

Table of Contents

EXCUSES, EXCUSES

Mr Krabs: Why did you bring your pet snail to work with you?

SpongeBob: He needs to come out of his shell.

Mrs Puff: Why don't you get As and Bs?

SpongeBob: I want to be a "sea" student!

Mr Krabs: Why did you miss work yesterday?

Squidward: I didn't miss it at all!

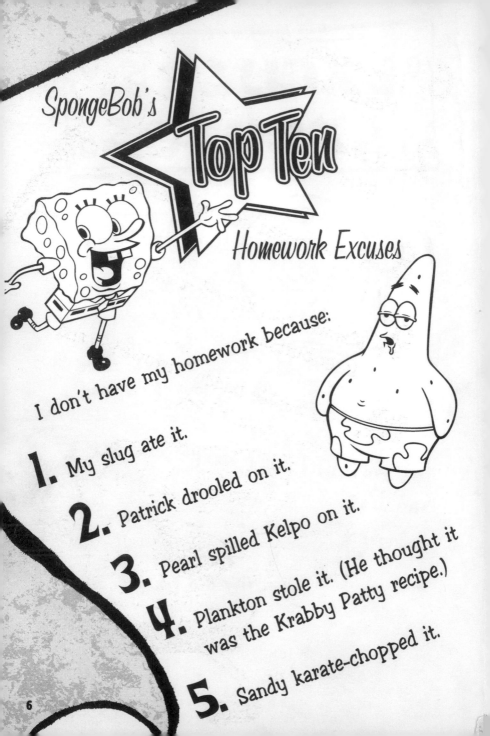

SpongeBob's Top Ten

Homework Excuses

I don't have my homework because:

1. My slug ate it.

2. Patrick drooled on it.

3. Pearl spilled Kelpo on it.

4. Plankton stole it. (He thought it was the Krabby Patty recipe.)

5. Sandy karate-chopped it.

6. It was eaten by Nematodes.

7. It was swallowed by giant clams.

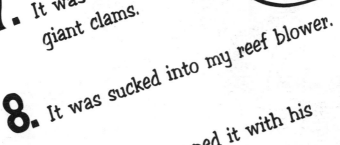

8. It was sucked into my reef blower.

9. Mermaidman zapped it with his laser button.

10. My bubble buddy borrowed it and never gave it back.

SpongeBob:
There were two
cookies in the jar
last night, and
this morning
there's only one.
How do you
explain that?

Patrick: It was so
dark, I guessed I
missed it!

Mrs Puff: Why did you go jellyfishing instead of writing your book report?

SpongeBob: Book report? I thought you said, "Brook report!"

Mr Krabs: Why do you keep stealing the Krabby Patty recipe?

Plankton: I'd buy it from you, but I'm a little short.

SPONGEBOB'S Top Ten EXCUSES

FOR FLUNKING THE DRIVING EXAM AGAIN

1. I forgot to wear my lucky underwear.

2. I swerved to avoid a killer guppy.

3. I thought it was "Opposite Day," so I tried to do everything wrong.

4. I enjoy the test so much, I'm hoping to take it thirty-nine more times!

5. I didn't feel well—I had a haddock.

6. I stopped when I heard the seaweed yelling, "Kelp! Kelp!"

7. I could hardly hear Patrick on the walkie-talkie.

Can you help SpongeBob come up with three more excuses?

Write them here:

8. _____

9. _____

10. _____

Mrs Puff: Why are you always late for school?

SpongeBob: They're always ringing the bell before I get here!

Mr Krabs: Why do you always get in trouble?

SpongeBob: Once I get in, it's hard to get out.

Why didn't Mrs Puff
believe the Flying
Dutchman's excuse?

She could see right through it.

Mr Krabs: Why are
you so behind in
Krabby Patty orders?

SpongeBob: I don't know, but
I'm trying to ketchup!

SpongeBob: Why can't you ever stand still?

Sandy: IF I do, I'll go nuts.

Teacher: Why are you putting on lipstick in class?

Pearl: I thought it was a make-up exam!

Squidward: Why can't you leave me alone?

SpongeBob and Patrick: You're our favourite stick-in-the-sand.

SpongeBob's  Top Ten Excuses

For Being Late to Work

1. I had to match my athletic socks to my uniform.

2. I had to blow some very important bubbles.

3. I had to help Mermaidman catch Man Ray.

4. I had to recharge my shell phone.

5. I had to walk the snail.

6. I was waiting for the piano tuna.

7. My foghorn alarm clock broke.

8. I had to cheer up a blue whale.

9. I woke up on the wrong side of the pineapple.

10. I'm actually early for work— tomorrow!

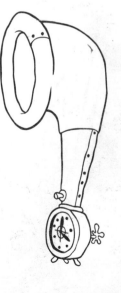

KARATE CUTS

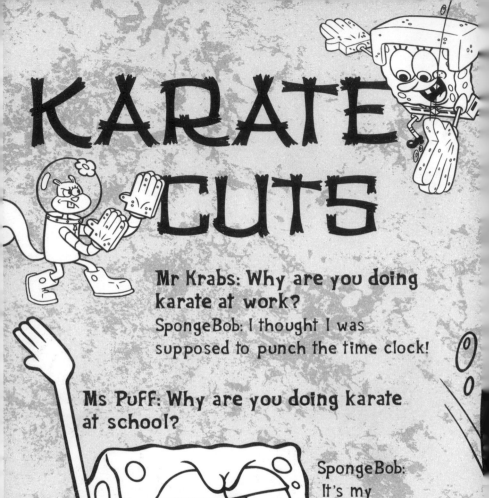

Mr Krabs: Why are you doing karate at work?

SpongeBob: I thought I was supposed to punch the time clock!

Ms Puff: Why are you doing karate at school?

SpongeBob: It's my back-to-school chopping!

Squidward: Why are you doing karate in the kitchen?

SpongeBob: I wanted to show I could cut the mustard!

Squidward: Why are you blowing bubbles?

SpongeBob: Because I already blew my nose.

Salty Answers to Stupid Questions

Customer: Do you sell Krabby Patties?
Squidward: No, we make them laugh. They're very picklish.

Squidward: Are you going jellyfishing?
SpongeBob and Patrick: No, we're catching some rays. Stingrays.

SpongeBob: Did you get into an accident?
Mrs Puff: No, I purposely crashed the
boat, so you would ask that question.

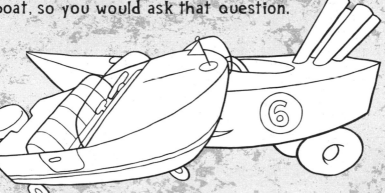

SpongeBob: Are you playing the clarinet?

Squidward: No, I'm
tickling it till it laughs.

Mr Krabs: Is that your pet snail?

SpongeBob: Shhhh! Mollusks are people, too, you know.

SpongeBob: Are you asleep?

Patrick: No, I'm using my body to hold this rock down.

SALTY ANSWERS at the Krusty Krab

Customer: There's a Fly on my Krabby Patty!

Squidward: Don't worry, we won't charge you extra for it.

Customer: Are Krabby Patties healthy?

Squidward: I've never heard one complain.

Customer: Will my Krabby Patty be long?

Squidward: No, it'll be round, sir.

Customer: This Krabby Patty tastes funny.

Squidward: Then why aren't you laughing?

Customer: Do you have seaweed salad on the menu?

Squidward: No, I wiped it off!

Mr Krabs: How'd you find your Krabby Patty, mate?

Customer: Easy. I just moved the Fries, and there it was!

Even More Excuses

Mr Krabs: Why did you spill sea onion ice cream on your new Krusty Krab uniform?

SpongeBob: My old one was in the laundry!

Pearl: Daddy, why aren't you paying attention?

Mr Krabs: Um . . . how much do I have to pay it?

Mrs Puff: Why are you raising your hand before I'm finished?

SpongeBob: I'm not! I'm hailing a crab.

Squidward: Can you dimwits keep down the noise? I can't even read!

Patrick: Too bad. I've been reading since I was a little starfish.

SpongeBob: Why don't you take the garbage out?

Patrick: We don't like the same movies!

NOTES FROM THE UNDERGROUND

Ahoy, teacher!
Please excuse my darlin'
Pearl from gym class.
She hurt her fin carrying
a bucket o'clams at the
Krusty Krab.

So she shouldn't
be asked to
do any kind
of exercise,
except cheerleading
practise. Or I'll sue
for ever'thing you've got.

Yours truly,
Mr Krabs

Dear Mrs Puff,

Please excuse my bubble
buddy from missing school.
He was nervous about the
"pop" quiz.

From now on, he'll try not
to be absent.

SpongeBob

from the desk of **Mrs Puff**

SpongeBob,

I'll give your bubble buddy another chance, but frankly I don't know what you see in him. . . .

Mrs Puff

Dear Mr Krabs,
Please excuse SpongeBob for
missing work, but he has been
struck down by the dreaded
Suds, which cause sniffling,
sneezing, and complaining.

He must stay in bed for three
days, drink plenty of Diet Dr.
Kelp, and watch *Mermaidman
and Barnacleboy.* This is the
only known cure.

Sincerely,
Dr. Fishman

Dear Mrs Puff,

My daughter couldn't take her boating exam because she was just too chicken.

Henrietta Hen

from the desk of **Mrs Puff**

Eggs-cuses, eggs-cuses!

—Mrs Puff

Patrick's mum: Patrick brought a note home from school.

Patrick's dad: What did it say?

Patrick's mum: They want a written excuse for his presence.

Patrick: The snail ate my homework.

Mrs Puff: But you don't have a snail!

Patrick: It was a stray!

Sandy: Why are you wearing fake muscles?

SpongeBob: The muscles are real – the rest of me is fake.

SPONGEBOB'S Top Ten EXCUSES

FOR LOSING THE KRUSTY KRAB TALENT SHOW

1. My hands were clammy.

2. Choosing socks that match is a talent!

3. Squidward's better since he switched to electric clarinet.

4. I didn't know Patrick could carry a tuna!

5. I shouldn't have agreed to do a ballet with Plankton.

6. My pineapple's too crowded for more trophies.

7. I can't compete with Patrick - he's a star!

8. I didn't know that was the judge's head.

Can you help SpongeBob come up with two more excuses?

Write them here:

9. _____

10. _____

Pearl: Why is money so important to you?

Mr Krabs: Who ay it'$ $o important?

Policeman: Did you see that sign that said *ONE WAY*?

Patrick: But Officer, I'm only going one way!

Mrs Puff: Why are you late for the first day of school?

SpongeBob: My clock was slow.

Mrs Puff: Do you expect me to believe that?

SpongeBob: You'd be slow, too, if you were running all night.

Mix 'n' Match 'n' EXCUSE ME!

First match a character in Column A with a problem in Column B. Then on the next few pages write an excuse for that character!

Column A

SpongeBob

Squidward

Patrick

Mr Krabs

Pearl

Plankton

Mrs Puff

Sandy

Column B

waking up late

missing an appointment

losing a shoe

forgetting to make dinner

burning a Krabby Patty

spilling food on a Krusty Krab customer

not writing a thank-you note for a birthday gift

driving too fast

Excuses

1. _____ 's excuse for
    (character)

_____ is: _____
    (problem)

_____.
    (excuse)

2. _____ 's excuse for
    (character)

_____ is: _____
    (problem)

_____.
    (excuse)

3. _____'s excuse
(character)

for_____
(problem)

is: _____
(excuse)

_____.

4. _____'s
(character)

excuse for _____

_____
(problem)

is: _____
(excuse)

_____.

5. _____'s excuse for _____
(character)

_____
(problem)

is: _____.
(excuse)

6._____ 's excuse for
　　　(character)

_____ is: _____.
　　(problem)　　　　　　　　　　　　(excuse)

7._____ 's excuse for
　　　(character)

_____ is: _____.
　　(problem)　　　　　　　　　　　　(excuse)

8._____ 's excuse for
　　　(character)

_____
　　(problem)

_____

is:_____
　　　(excuse)

_____

_____.

SPONGEBOB'S EXCUSE FOR WRITING THIS BOOK

No one else would write it for me!

THE END